The
Supermarket
Mice

First published in the U.S.A. 1984 by E. P. Dutton, Inc.,
2 Park Avenue, New York, N.Y. 10016

First published in Great Britain by Kestrel Books, 1984

Printed in Great Britain   ISBN 0-525-44145-X

10 9 8 7 6 5 4 3 2 1   OBE   First Edition

Margaret Gordon

The Supermarket Mice

E. P. Dutton · New York

In a town there was a street.

In the street there was a supermarket.

In the supermarket worked

Trevor,   Sidney   and   Mabel.

Some mice also worked in the supermarket,

and they lived there as well,

in great comfort behind the shelves.

Trevor, Sidney and Mabel looked
after the supermarket by day,

and the supermarket mice looked after it
at night.

One day Trevor noticed a packet of crackers nibbled at the corner.

"Phoebe, how could you be so careless?"
said Mrs. Mouse.

The next day Sidney noticed some rice
falling out of a little hole in a bag.

"How naughty of you, James," said
Mr. Mouse.

The day after that, Mabel saw a mouse.

"Oh no," said Mr. and Mrs. Mouse.

"We must get a cat," said Trevor.

"My mom's got a cat," said Sidney.

"Get that cat," said Mabel.

"Oh help," said all the mice.

So Sidney brought his mom's cat.
He was called Bounce and was very fat.

"Could be worse," said Mr. Mouse.

"Take care tonight," said Mrs. Mouse.

So that night the mice took great care

to make friends with the cat.

They discovered he ate anything

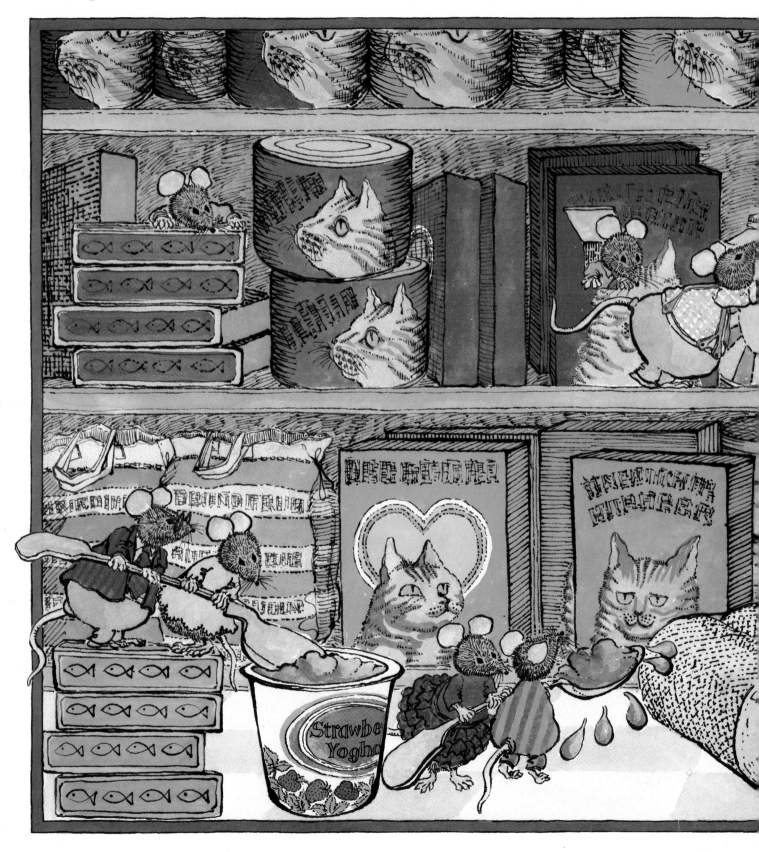

and everything.

After that night, Bounce the cat
always cleared up after the mice.
All was tidy when Trevor, Mabel and Sidney
arrived in the morning.

"No nibbled crackers today," said Trevor.

"No rice on the floor today," said Sidney.

"No mice," said Mabel.

"Thank goodness we got that cat," they said.

"Thank GOODNESS we've got that cat," said the mice.